UPSIDE-DOWN
SID

DYLAN SHEARSBY is a storyboard artist and
illustrator, as well as a painter and teacher of watercolor.
Upside-Down Sid is his first picture book, for which he
took inspiration from childhood favorites Postman Pat
and La Linea. Dylan lives in Australia with his wife and
Wolfgang the cat.

First American Edition 2019
Kane Miller, A Division of EDC Publishing

Copyright © Dylan Shearsby 2018

First published in Australia in 2018 by Little Hare Books, an imprint of Hardie Grant Egmont

For information contact:
Kane Miller, A Division of EDC Publishing
P.O. Box 470663
Tulsa, OK 74147-0663
www.kanemiller.com
www.edcpub.com
www.usbornebooksandmore.com

Library of Congress Control Number: 2018958224

Printed and bound in China
1 2 3 4 5 6 7 8 9 10
ISBN: 978-1-61067-889-6

Dec19
J
PIC

UPSIDE-DOWN SID

Written and illustrated by Dylan Shearsby

Kane Miller
A DIVISION OF EDC PUBLISHING

In a town much like yours, where everything
is the right side up ...

lived Upside-Down Sid.

and he was the other.

With a few small exceptions.

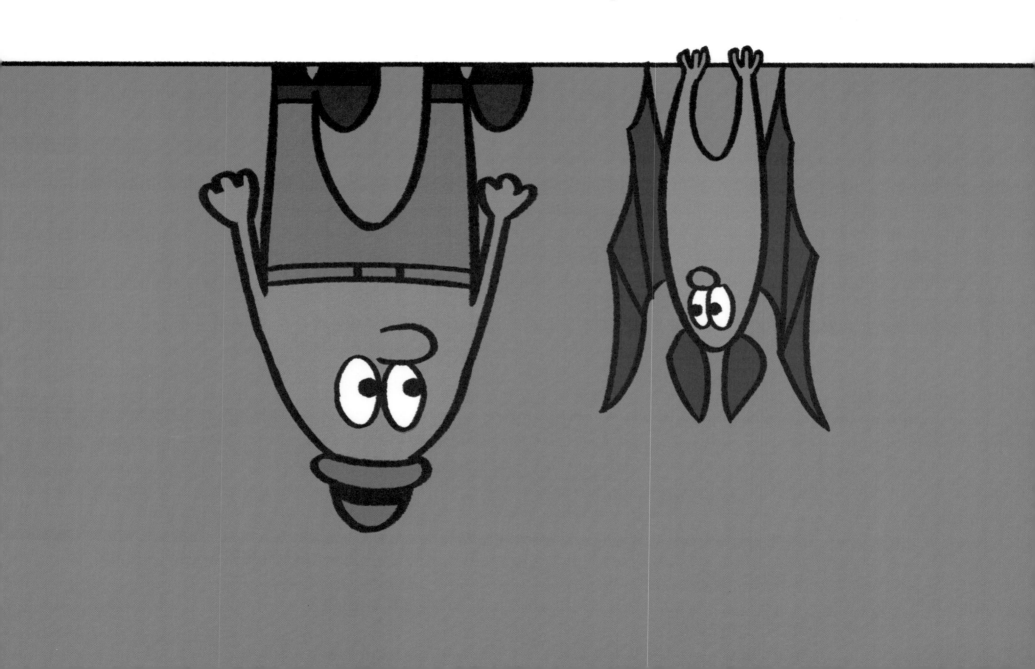

Sid tried not to let it bother him.

But it wasn't easy fitting in ...

or making friends.

Sid looked forward to his quiet time at home.

It was the one place he could go about his
business without too much fuss.

Yet there were days he wished he had help ...

and company.

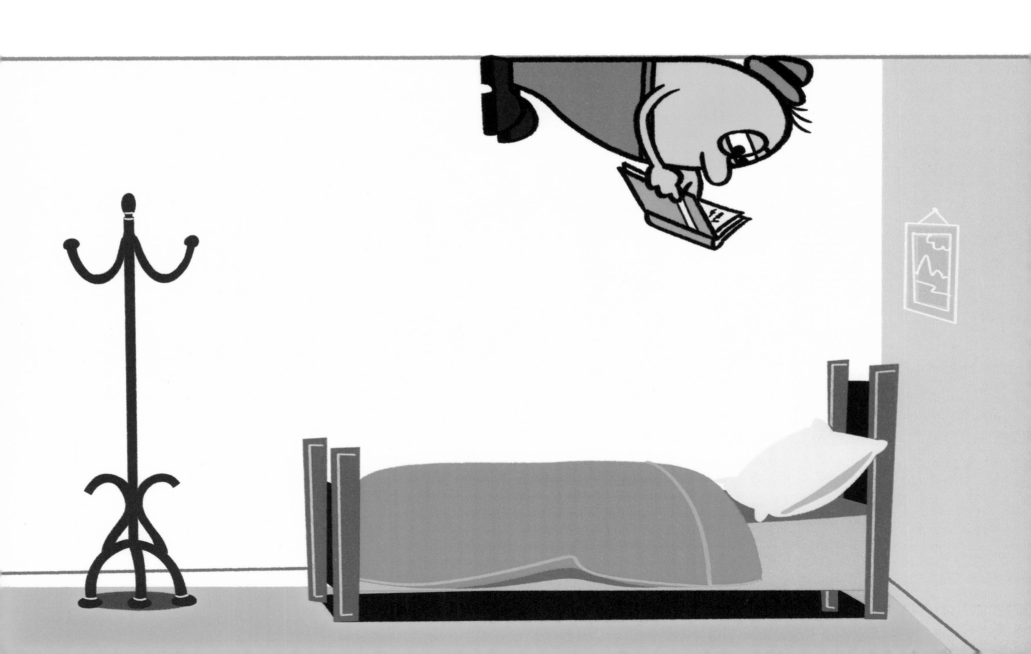

One morning, while Sid was eating his breakfast,
a basketball smashed through his window.

"Sorry!" came a voice from outside. "We'll fix it," said his neighbor. "And we'll make it up to you," said another.

Sid's neighbors bought him a ticket to the fairground.
But Sid wasn't allowed on the roller coaster.

And, in the haunted house, it was Sid who frightened the ghosts!

Sid was ready to go home. "Would you like to come over for lunch?" he asked.
"Yes, please!" they all said.

On the way home, Sid began to feel nervous.

He soon realized he was in over his head.

"That was a lunch to remember!" said his neighbors.
Sid wondered if he'd ever see them again.

The next morning, as Sid left the house, his neighbors were waiting out of sight.

When he was gone, they went inside
with their tools and ladders.

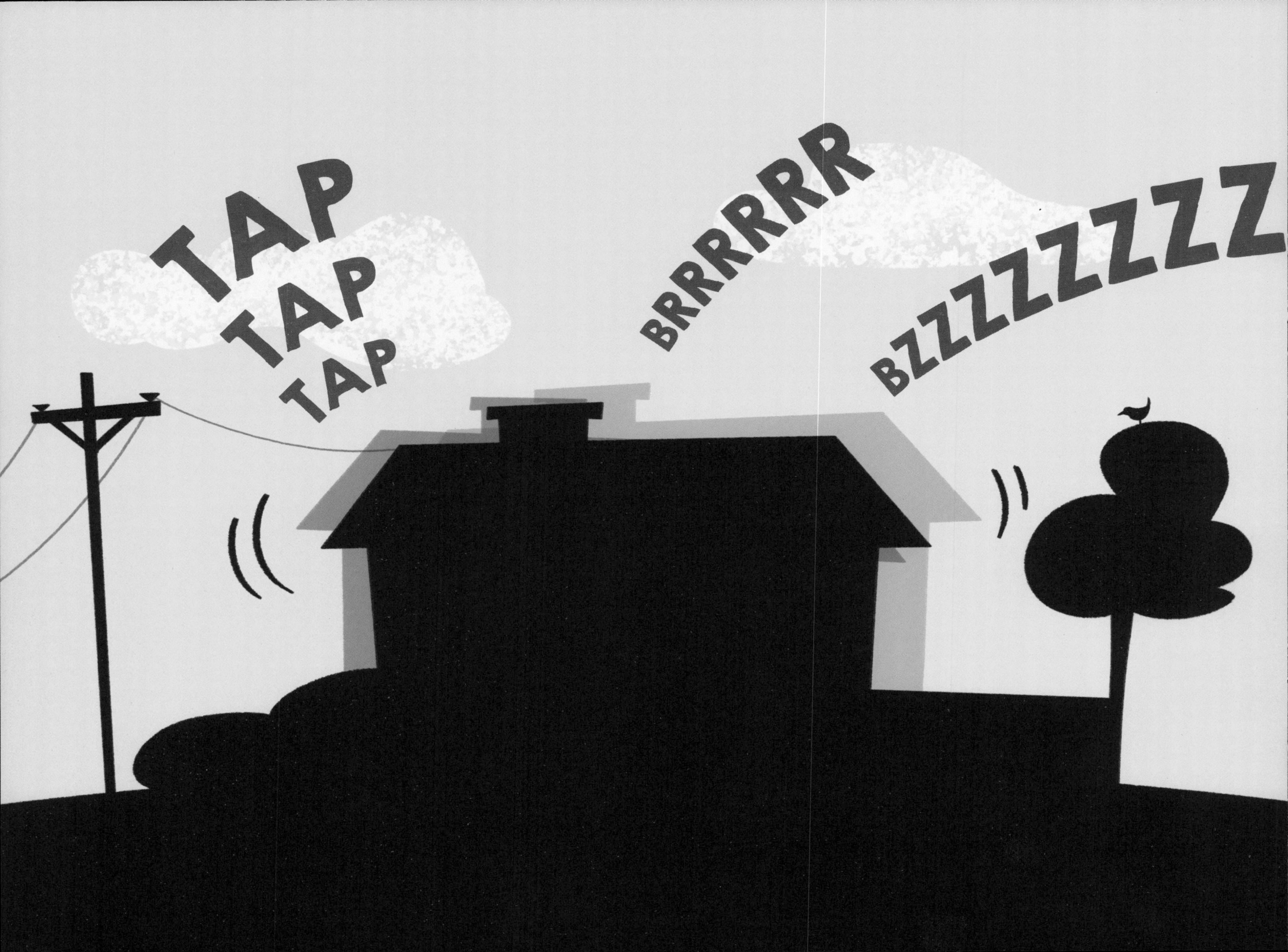
TAP
TAP
TAP
BRRRRRR
BZZZZZZZZ

When Sid arrived home later that day, he noticed his window had been fixed. *Look at that!* he thought.

He flopped onto his couch and looked around. Something felt odd.

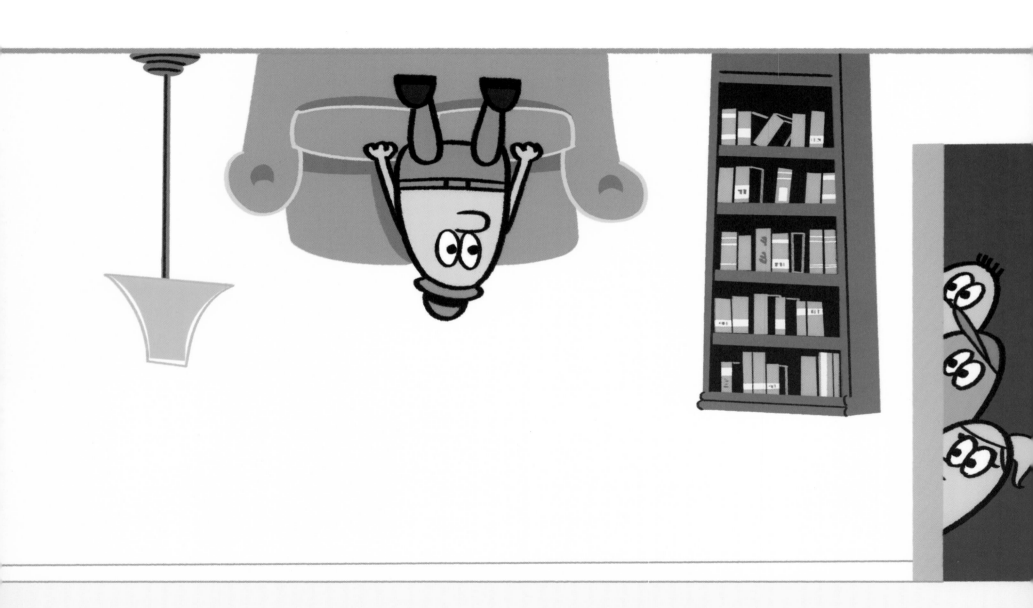

"Wait a minute!" he said. "My couch, my bookcase ...
EVERYTHING is my way up!"

This called for a special upside-down party!

That night, for the very first time, Sid climbed into his bed and fell asleep.

And he *did* see his friends again, almost every day.